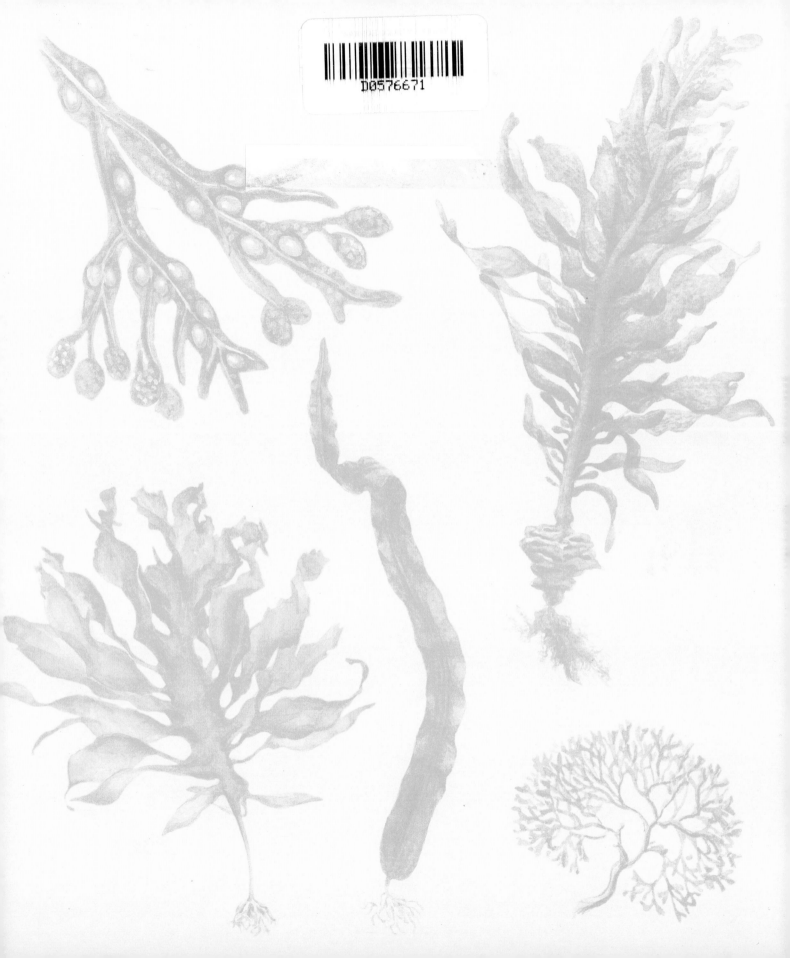

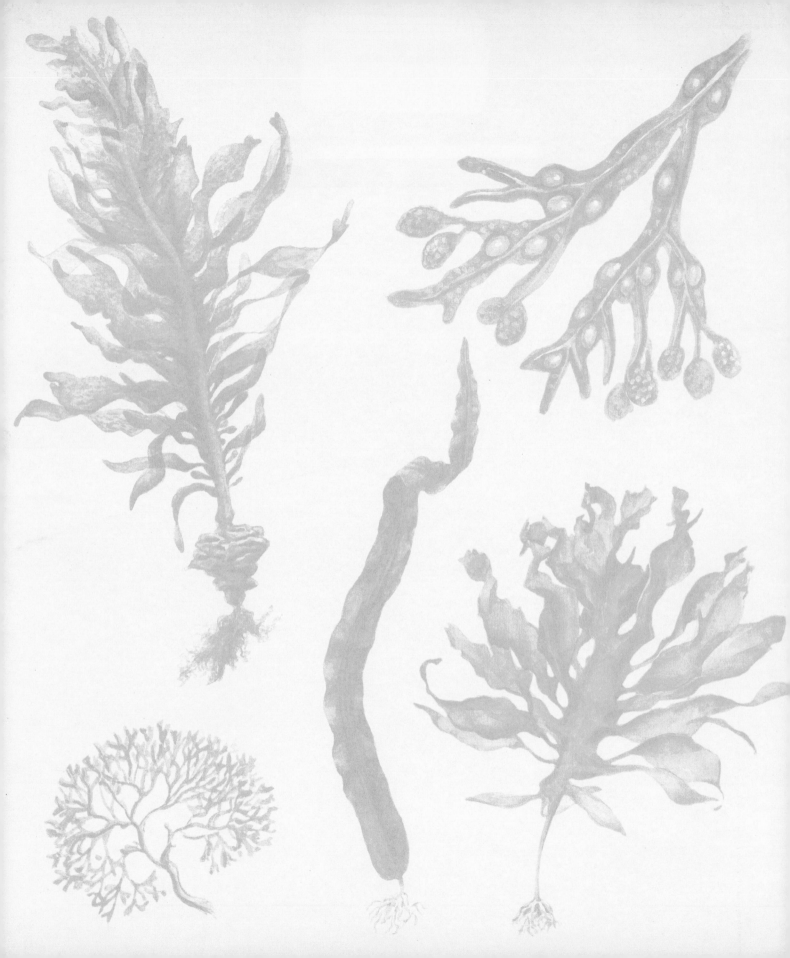

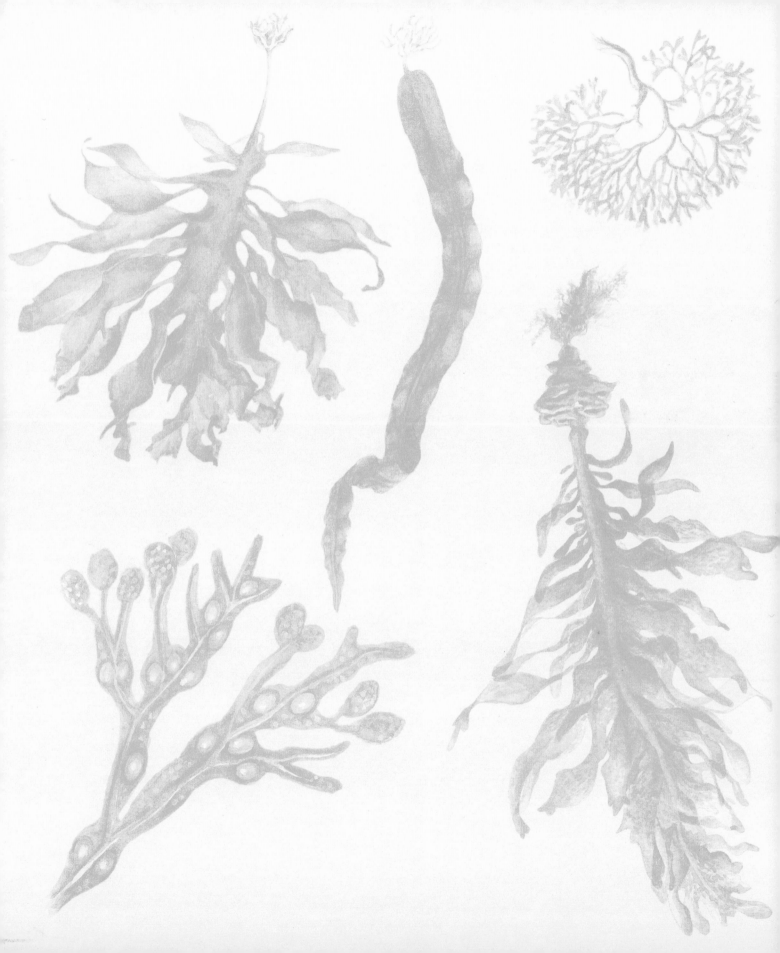

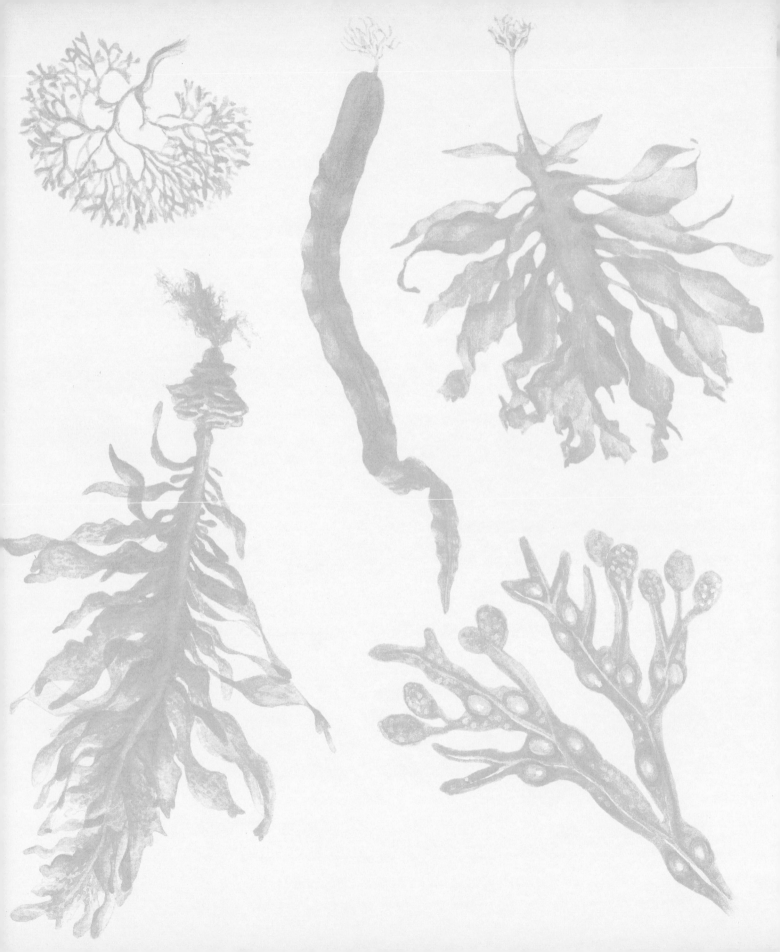

Library of Congress Cataloging-in-Publication Data

Thompson, Holly.
  The wakame gatherers / by Holly Thompson ; illustrated by Kazumi
Wilds.
    p. cm.
  Summary: When Nanami's Gram from Maine visits Japan, Nanami's
Japanese grandmother, Baachan, takes them to the seashore to gather
wakame seaweed. Includes several recipes for wakame.
  ISBN 978-1-885008-33-6
  [1. Grandmothers--Fiction. 2. Seaweed--Fiction. 3. Japan--Fiction.] I.
Wilds, Kazumi Inose, ill. II. Title.

PZ7.T3715925Wak 2007
[E]--dc22
                    2007027947

Shen's Books
Walnut Creek, California

SHEN'S BOOKS

Printed in China

Book Design and computer production:
Patty Arnold, *Menagerie Design and Publishing*

Wakame Recipes

NANAMI'S WAKAME SALAD

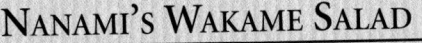

Make a salad with your favorite greens and sliced vegetables. Rehydrate 2 tablespoons of chopped wakame and drain. Sprinkle wakame and toasted sesame seeds over the salad. Dress the salad with one of the following dressings:

Dressing 1: your favorite bottled dressing

Dressing 2: 2 Tbsp. Japanese soy sauce + 2 Tbsp. lemon or lime juice, mixed together

Dressing 3: 2 Tbsp. rice vinegar + 1 Tbsp. sesame oil + 1 tsp. sugar, mixed together

BAACHAN'S WAKAME MISO SOUP

    3 c. dashi* stock

    1 Tbsp. miso (any type)

    2 Tbsp. dried, chopped wakame, rehydrated

    1/2 block of tofu, chopped into 1/2-inch cubes

    1/4 c. scallion or chives, chopped fine

Heat dashi stock in a saucepan. Ladle some of the hot stock into a bowl; dissolve the miso in this, then add to the stock. Add the wakame and tofu, simmer, and turn off the heat as soon as tofu is heated—before the soup boils! Garnish with scallions or chives. Stir with chopsticks to eat.

* To make dashi or Japanese stock, soak a strip of konbu seaweed (about 3 inches long cut into 1-inch pieces) about 15 minutes in 3 cups of water. Heat to a boil, reduce heat, remove konbu and simmer for another 5 minutes. OR simply add 1 teaspoon dashi concentrate to 3 cups of water.

GRAM'S WAKAME LOBSTER SANDWICHES

    1 Tbsp. olive oil

    2 tsp. lemon juice

    salt and pepper to taste

    6-8 oz. cooked lobster or crab meat

    1 small avocado, pitted, peeled and sliced

    1-2 Tbsp. wakame, rehydrated, drained and cut into
        1-inch pieces

    lettuce leaves

    toasted bread or roll

In a bowl whisk together olive oil, lemon juice and salt and pepper. Add lobster, wakame and avocado. Make sandwiches with toasted bread, lettuce and lobster mixture. Eat outside!

All About Wakame

Seaweeds are large algae that grow in salt water all over the world. They are plants with leaf-like blades, a stem-like stipe, and a holdfast to hold tight to rocks. There are three main types of seaweed: green, brown and red. Wakame is a brown seaweed, but when boiled, it changes color to bright green.

Although many cultures do not eat seaweeds or sea vegetables, people in Japan and Korea have been eating seaweeds for centuries. Many Japanese go to the shore like Nanami to gather seaweeds in spring. The Latin name for wakame is *Undaria pinnatifida*—it is one of the most commonly eaten seaweeds in Japan. In the past, only naturally growing wakame was eaten, but now wakame is cultivated on ropes in the open sea and harvested several months later. Seaweeds don't really produce seeds; they produce spores, and when Nanami is older she will help tie little sporelings onto the ropes for growing wakame.

In Japan, fresh wakame can be found in markets from early spring into summer. Dried wakame is available year-round. In North America, wakame can be found in Asian and natural food stores (the Atlantic equivalent of wakame is *alaria*).

Dried wakame needs to be soaked in lukewarm water for about 20 minutes to be rehydrated; it will swell to about twice its size! After soaking, cut away any midrib or other tough sections (not necessary if your wakame is the chopped variety). If you want your wakame to turn bright green, drop it into boiling water, then remove with tongs or a slotted spoon and quickly rinse in cold water. You can also drop chopped wakame into soup just before serving. Wakame is high in nutrients and should not be boiled or simmered for more than a minute, or it will lose these important nutrients. Wakame has a nice crisp texture and is delicious in soups and salads.

Wakame

Konbu

Kajime

Irish Moss

Rockweed

Nanami's Glossary

JAPANESE	PRONUNCIATION	ENGLISH
Baachan	(BAH-chahn)	grandmother (familiar)
daijobu	(die-JO-boo)	okay, safe, clear of danger
gomen nasai	(go-men nah-sigh)	I'm sorry
konbu	(KON-boo)	konbu, kombu, kelp (*Laminaria* species)
kajime	(KAH-jee-may)	kajime seaweed (*Ecklonia cava*)
monpe	(MON-pay)	work pants gathered at the ankles
mottainai	(moat-TIE-nigh)	wasteful, too good to waste
nori	(NO-ree)	nori, laver (*Porphyra* species)
ponzu	(PON-zoo)	sauce of citrus juice and soy sauce
sakana	(sah-kah-nah)	fish
senso	(sen-soh)	war
wakame	(wah-kah-may)	wakame (*Undaria pinnatifida*)
yatta!	(yaht-TAH)	(I/we/you/she, etc.) did it!

I whoop with excitement. Baachan has never been to Maine.

"Translate!" Baachan says impatiently.

As I change Gram's words into Japanese, I pull the plane tickets from the envelope. Baachan touches the printed letters and numbers and blinks with tears. She has never been on an airplane. She has never left Japan.

I take her hand and raise it into the air.

"*Daijobu!*" I say. "*Daijobu!*"

Dear Hatsumi,

Here are your tickets. I hope
you can come. I will need some
help from you and Nanami
pulling lobster traps this
summer.

Love,
Gram

I ask my mother what Gram's letter to Baachan
        says, but she tells me to take it to her. I hand the
        envelope to Baachan in the back garden. "Open
        it!" I say. Baachan washes her hands, dries them
        on her apron, then lifts the flap with her thumb.
        She pulls out a piece of notepaper. I read:

In April, three letters arrive in a packet from Gram. My mother reads hers, pulls out summer tickets for our flights to Maine and smiles; I know she is thinking of cold bays and quiet woods, seals. I open my letter:

Dear Nanami,

Yesterday I found wakame at a store in town! And bins of other dried seaweeds, too! Last night I made Hatsumi Baachan's wakame soup and today I made wakame lobster sandwiches. Now I will try to learn how to use the other seaweeds the store has. Some are harvested from the next bay over — alaria, kelp, even nori. Your Baachan was right. Such cold water — perfect for seaweed! Enclosed is a present for her.

Love, Gram

Later that morning, Baachan sets our biggest pot on the stove. We boil the wakame to green, just seconds, then remove it with tongs and plunge it into cold water. We save some wakame fresh in the refrigerator and take the rest to the laundry balcony to hang like socks. Baachan snips some ends with scissors, and as the day goes on we take turns unfurling the shriveling fronds to the sun. By the time the sun sets over the far mountains, our wakame has turned from silken to brittle black-green. The dried wakame will last for months in our cupboards.

For dinner we have fresh wakame with ponzu sauce, for breakfast wakame soup, and for lunch cucumber wakame salad.
A week later, when we take Gram to the airport to return to Maine, she has our dried wakame plus bagfuls bought from the fishing families tucked into her suitcase.

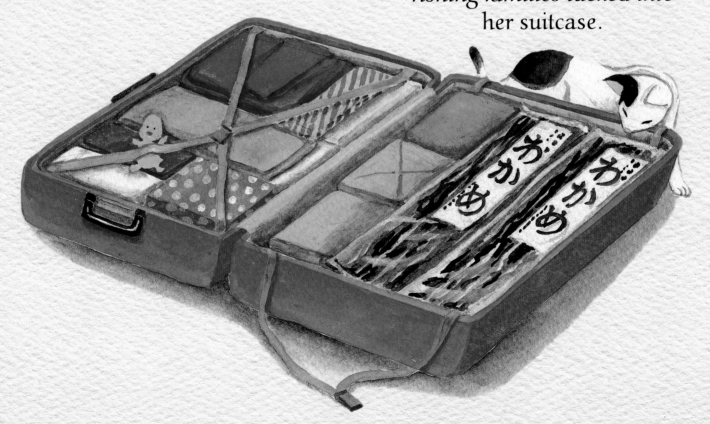

Then Gram takes my hand and raises it high. *"Daijobu!"* she shouts.

Baachan raises my other hand. *"Daijobu!"* she says.

And we all yell into the waves, *"Daijobu! Daijobu!"* Finally we return to wakame collecting.

I translate Baachan's words for Gram,
and my chin trembles as my grandmothers
nod and nod.

"I'm sorry," I finally say to one. "*Gomen nasai*," I say to the other.

Then Baachan surveys the waves, surfers, dog-walkers, people hanging seaweed by the breakwater and says, "Nanami-chan, always protect this peace."

"We came here often," Baachan says. "I didn't have much clothing.
    I never had boots. Most days I wore a simple kimono that had
    been mended many times, or a hand-me-down dress, or *monpe*.
    We were always hungry. But we were lucky to have the sea for fish
    and seaweed. Then my brother and I were sent into the mountains,
    to escape the bombs."

We all stand still in the noisy surf, wakame flapping from our waist bags.
    I gaze at the sky trying to imagine bombs raining. I know Baachan's
    mother died in a fire from those bombs.

"Tell me," Gram urges, so I take a deep breath and translate Baachan's
    words, understanding that when my grandmothers were my age they
    were enemies, their countries bombing each other's people.

I look from one grandmother to the other. I come from both of them,
    but I can't imagine parts of me at war with each other.

Then Baachan says, "*Nanami-chan, senso no toki datta wa yo.*" She nods for me to translate.

I hesitate then say, "It was the war time."

Gram nods knowingly.

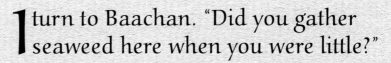turn to Baachan. "Did you gather seaweed here when you were little?"

"Of course. All kinds. Right at this beach."

I'm struck thinking of her as a young girl like me at this very spot. "And did you use your hands to grab wakame?" I ask.

"Of course!"

I translate for Gram then shake my head like a dog. My braids whip back and forth. "And did you do this with your hair?"

Baachan nods, and both grandmothers laugh.

"And did you have rain pants like these?"

Baachan stops hooking seaweed, sighs long and eyes me. I translate my question for Gram. They both look at me funny, but I know I'm using the right language with the right grandmother.

After a while, I stand and watch the surf.
Gram and Baachan are still gathering.
In some waves, cresting against the light,
schools of fish tumble. "*Sakana*!" I say,
"Fish!" and my grandmothers smile.

Gram is hooking seaweeds, too—brown, red and green. Then I point. "Wakame!" I shout. I untangle a frond wrapped around her legs and we stuff it into her bag. "*Yatta!*" I say. Gram stares. "*Yatta!*" I repeat. Then I realize I'm speaking Japanese. "We did it!" I say.

Soon I spy a curvy base in the waves and snag it with my bare hand. Then I leave my pole on the sand, enter the surf and use my hands to gather wakame. Without the pole, I'm fast, and my bag soon fills.

The waves crash hard against us. I use my pole, dipping down and pulling up when it feels heavy. I show Baachan.

"No, not wakame."

I hook more.

"No, that's *kajime*," she says. "No, konbu. Today we just want wakame."

We cross the breakwater and head toward the beach where surf slams on sand. Gram is amazed. In Maine snow still spots the ground, her bay is icy cold. Here, surfers ride waves, and the sun is strong.

We set down our buckets and bags and pull on rain pants and boots. Baachan hands us each a pole with a hooked end and steps into the water. She pokes at waves, pulls up clumps of seaweed, then tosses them aside. Finally, she nabs a long strand and calls us over.

"This is wakame," she says. "See the straight midrib? See the base all curvy?"

I translate, and we follow Baachan into the bay.

"We do!" Gram says. "Irish moss, rockweed,
bladderwrack, kelp. . ." I can't translate
these, so I tell Baachan there's lots of seaweed,
that I slip and fall on it when I explore the rocks
near Gram's house.

"But why don't they eat it?" Baachan asks.
"*Mottainai!*"—how wasteful!

I ask Gram why they don't eat the shaggy seaweed in
Maine.

"Well, rockweed's not so tasty," Gram says, "but we cook
lobsters in it. Remember?"

I describe this to Baachan, how in summer we layer rockweed
and lobsters in a pot over a fire on the beach.

But Baachan asks, "Isn't there any seaweed they eat?"

"Well, some people boil Irish moss for pudding," Gram
says, "and carrageenan is used in ice cream and
other foods. But we don't usually eat seaweed, as is,
in soup or salad. Though when I was a girl,
my father chewed dulse—a red seaweed."

"Strange," Baachan says after I translate.
"Such cold water, you always tell me.
Perfect for wakame and konbu."

Inside the breakwater, fishermen and women are hanging wakame. Steam rises from cauldrons. We stop to watch as men place long brown fronds into hot water. Like magic, the wakame instantly greens. They drop clumps of boiled wakame into buckets of cold water, lift cooled wakame into a crate, then carry the loads like laundry to lines for clipping. Waving in wind, the fronds look like silk scarves.

Gram is fascinated. She has never gathered seaweed for eating.

"Why?" asks Baachan when I translate. "In Maine you don't have seaweed?"

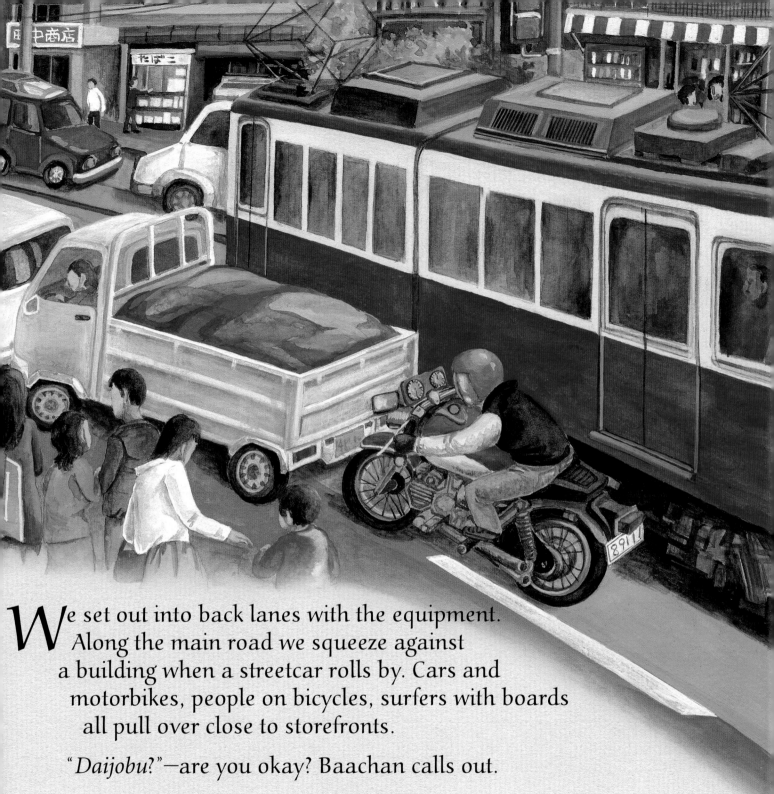

We set out into back lanes with the equipment.
Along the main road we squeeze against
a building when a streetcar rolls by. Cars and
motorbikes, people on bicycles, surfers with boards
all pull over close to storefronts.

"*Daijobu?*"—are you okay? Baachan calls out.

"*Daijobu!*"—okay! Gram says. *Daijobu* is one Japanese word
   Gram has learned.

The streetcar rumbles on, and everyone moves again.
   We follow Baachan toward the harbor.

Each spring, as warm winds are blowing, Baachan likes to gather wakame seaweed, and this year when Gram arrives for a visit during March break, Baachan asks Gram and me to help. Gram likes adventures, but I'm not so sure. This will be my first time out alone with Gram and Baachan, and I will be the only translator.

Baachan wakes us early one morning. She braids my hair with her fast fingers then goes out to the shed.

"Wakame doesn't just grow on rocks on the sea floor," I tell Gram as we eat breakfast rice and soup. "It grows on ropes the fishermen set. Next year, with my class, I'll help seed those ropes." Between slurps, I tell how "seeds" grow into fronds, then ropes are pulled up and the wakame harvested. Now the rope harvest is nearly finished, and fishermen take boats out to where wakame grows naturally and cut fronds with long poles and blades. Some washes ashore, and Baachan knows just where to go to find that wakame and fronds pounded loose by waves.

"We'll get wet," Baachan says from the doorway where she's gathered buckets, poles, plastic bags and boots. I translate, and Gram gives a thumbs-up.

Gram's town in Maine surrounds a bay
with rocky shores, quiet with woods.
I visit in summers and swim in
the cold Atlantic. At low tide,
the rocks are seaweed shaggy
with green crabs hiding
beneath. Sometimes we
pull lobster traps in
the bay, and seals
poke their heads
up to study us.

My name is Nanami—Seven Seas—and I have
two grandmothers from two different seas:
Gram from Maine, and Baachan,
who lives with us here in Japan.

Baachan's town, my town, rims a bay with
sandy beaches and surfers. A streetcar
runs between shops, houses, temples
and shrines, and near our home
is a harbor where fishing
families hang seaweed
and set racks of
fish to dry.

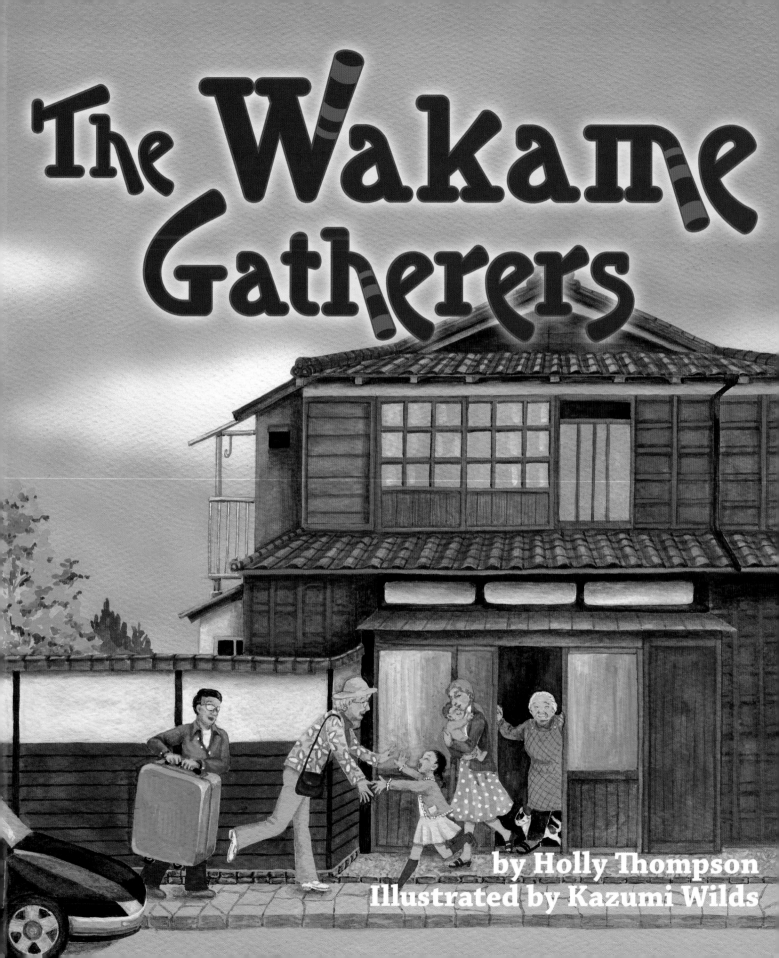

The Wakame Gatherers

by Holly Thompson

Illustrated by Kazumi Wilds